DORA saves the SNOW PRINCESS

adapted by Phoebe Beinstein illustrated by Dave Aikins

Simon Spotlight/Nick Jr.
New York London Toronto Sydney

Based on the TV series *Dora the Explorer*® as seen on Nick Jr.®

SIMON SPOTLIGHT
An imprint of Simon & Schuster Children's Publishing Division
1230 Avenue of the Americas, New York, New York 10020

Manufactured in the United States of America
20 19 18 17 16 15
ISBN-13: 978-1-4169-5866-6
ISBN-10: 1-4169-5866-5
0110 LAK

¡Hola! Today I'm reading a book to all my friends. Do you like books? We love books! Boots, Tico, Benny, and Isa really want to hear a story about a snow princess, a witch, and a snow fairy. Do you see a story like that?

Once upon a time there was a little girl named Sabrina who loved snow. Sabrina lived in a lonely, dry forest where it never snowed. One day during a walk, she saw a little white dove sitting in a tree, crying.

"What's wrong?" Sabrina asked the dove.

"I'm caught in a trap set by a mean witch, but no one will free me because they're all afraid of her." The dove showed Sabrina his trapped foot.

"I'll free you!" said Sabrina, and she helped him out of the trap.

"You are very kind and brave," the dove said. "You must be the one! Follow me. I have something special to show you." The white dove led Sabrina to several bushes. "It's behind the bush with the purple berries," said the dove.

Sabrina looked behind the bush and saw something beautiful sticking out of the ground.

"It's a magic crystal!" the dove said. "Now look into it and smile."

So Sabrina did, and the most amazing thing happened.

It started to snow! Then Sabrina became the Snow Princess and the white dove became the Snow Fairy.

"Me, a princess?" Sabrina asked.

"Yes. The forest was under the Witch's spell, but because of your bravery and kindness all the snow animals are free!" said the Snow Fairy.

Everyone in the forest was very happy, until one day the Snow Princess saw the Witch flying in the sky. The Witch suddenly swooped down and grabbed the crystal out of the Snow Princess's hand. She made a mean face into the crystal to stop the snow, and then locked the Snow Princess in the top of a tower.

"Now it will never snow again. Ha! Ha! Ha!" said the Witch before she flew away.

The snow in the forest began to melt. The animals looked for the Snow Princess, but they didn't see her anywhere, so they asked the Snow Fairy to find her. The Snow Fairy knew he didn't have much time before everything melted.

Look! The Snow Fairy is flying right out of the story! He thinks I'm the Snow Princess!

Hi, Snow Fairy! I'm not the Snow Princess, but I think we can help you find her because we know where she is—in the tower! Let's jump into the book and help the Snow Fairy find her. Are you ready to jump? Jump, jump, jump!

Now we need to find out where the tower is. Who do we ask for help when we don't know which way to go? Yeah, Map! Map says we need to go across the Icy Ocean, past the Snow Hills, and through the cave. Then we'll reach the tower.

I see the Icy Ocean down this big hill. Benny's pulling a sled that we can ride on.

Oh, no. I see that sneaky fox, Swiper. He's going to swipe the Snow Fairy! Quick, say "Swiper, no swiping! Swiper, no swiping! Swiper, no swiping!"

Good job! You stopped Swiper.

Here we are at the Icy Ocean, but we need a boat to go across. Look, there's the Pirate Piggies' ship! We love the Pirate Piggies. Will you help us call them? Say "Pirate Piggies!"

They're coming to help us. Let's get on their ship! Watch out for icebergs!

Look! That iceberg isn't an iceberg. It's an icy sea snake coming right towards us! The Witch must have done this. But the Pirate Piggies know just how to scare an icy sea snake. All you have to do is yell "Arrrrrrg!" really loud. Will you be a pirate and help us scare the snake? Ready? Yell "Arrrrrrg!" Wow, what a great pirate you are!

Yay! The Pirate Piggies got us across the ocean and we found a snow hill, but Boots says this snow hill is moving. Wait . . . this isn't a snow hill. Snow Fairy says that the Witch turned the hill into a polar bear! Does the polar bear look happy or angry? Angry? Uh-oh. We'd better run!

There's a girl with a dog sled. Maybe she can help us!

Her name is Paj. Paj says she can take us away from the polar bear and right to the cave.

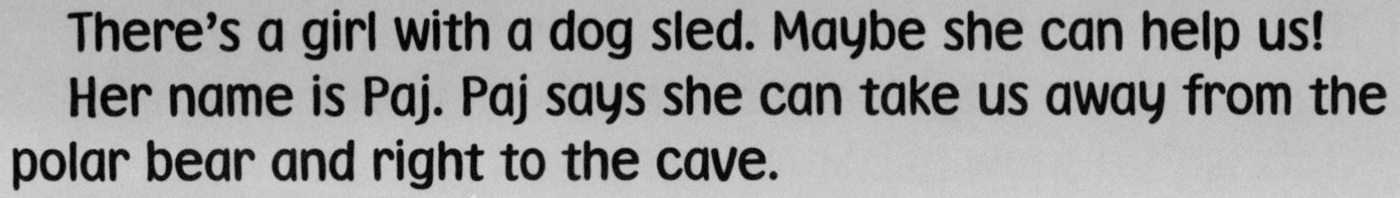

Wow, Paj's dogs run fast! To get around the hills, we have to lean. Will you lean left? Great! Now let's lean to the right. Good leaning! Paj and her dogs helped us get away from the polar bear and brought us to the cave.

This cave is really dark. Do you see a way out? Yeah, up there! Let's climb up and out.

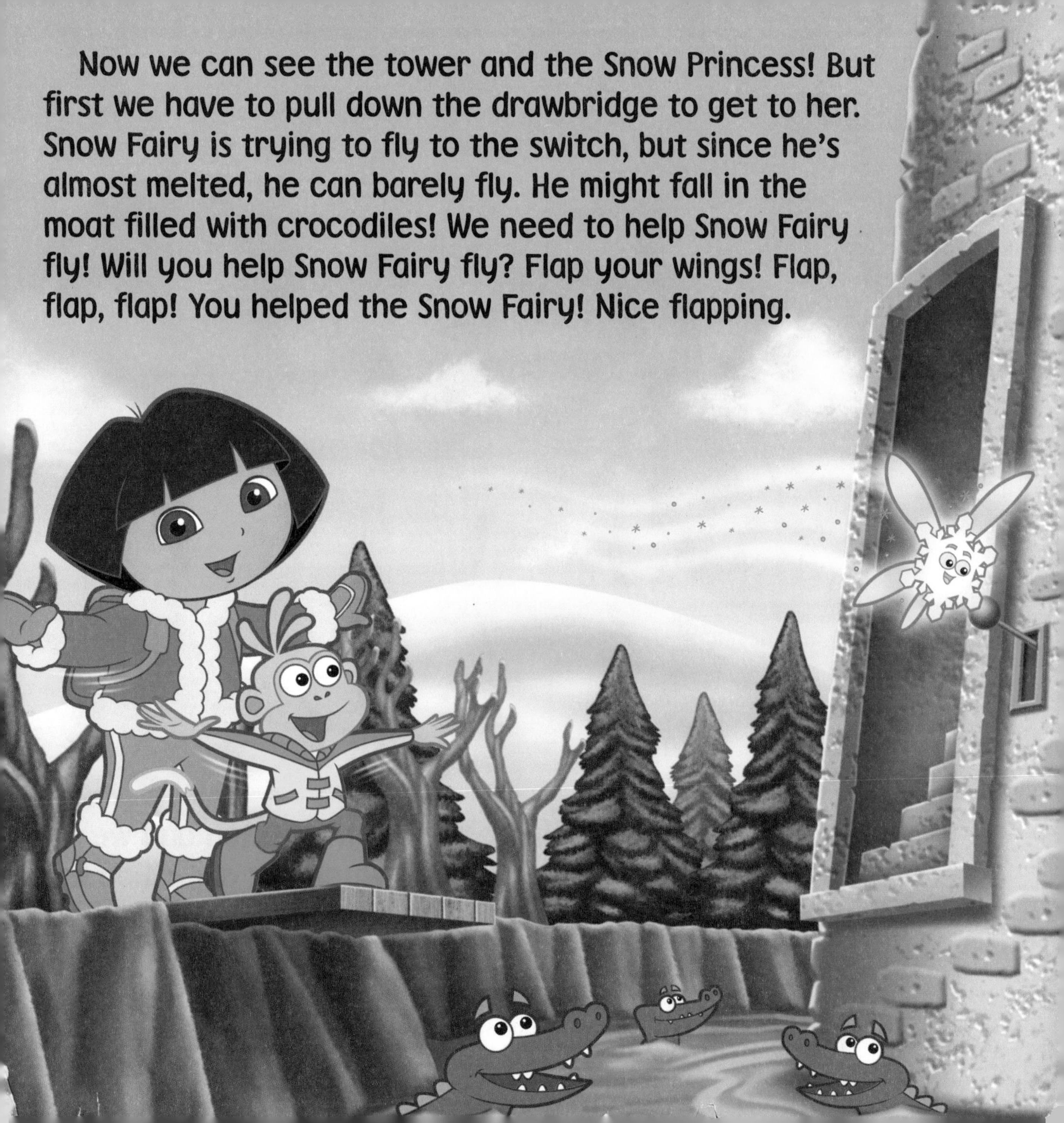

Now we can see the tower and the Snow Princess! But first we have to pull down the drawbridge to get to her. Snow Fairy is trying to fly to the switch, but since he's almost melted, he can barely fly. He might fall in the moat filled with crocodiles! We need to help Snow Fairy fly! Will you help Snow Fairy fly? Flap your wings! Flap, flap, flap! You helped the Snow Fairy! Nice flapping.

Snow Fairy was able to fly all the way to the switch and we reached the Snow Princess. She says the Witch put a spell on her and now she can't smile. If she can't smile into the crystal then it won't snow and everything will melt.

I see the Witch coming now! Maybe I can pretend to be the Snow Princess and smile into the crystal. You can help me smile too.

Now I look just like the Snow Princess! The Witch thinks I'm the princess and that I can't smile, but do we have a surprise for her! We'd better hurry before everything melts. Will you help me smile into the crystal? *¡Uno, dos, tres!* SMILE!

We did it! Our smiles made it snow again, and the Witch lost her powers forever! Now the Magic Snowy Forest is safe!

The Snow Fairy dressed us all like princesses and princes. But anyone can feel like a prince or a princess if they're kind and brave and like to help friends! Thanks for being kind and brave and helping us. *¡Adiós!*